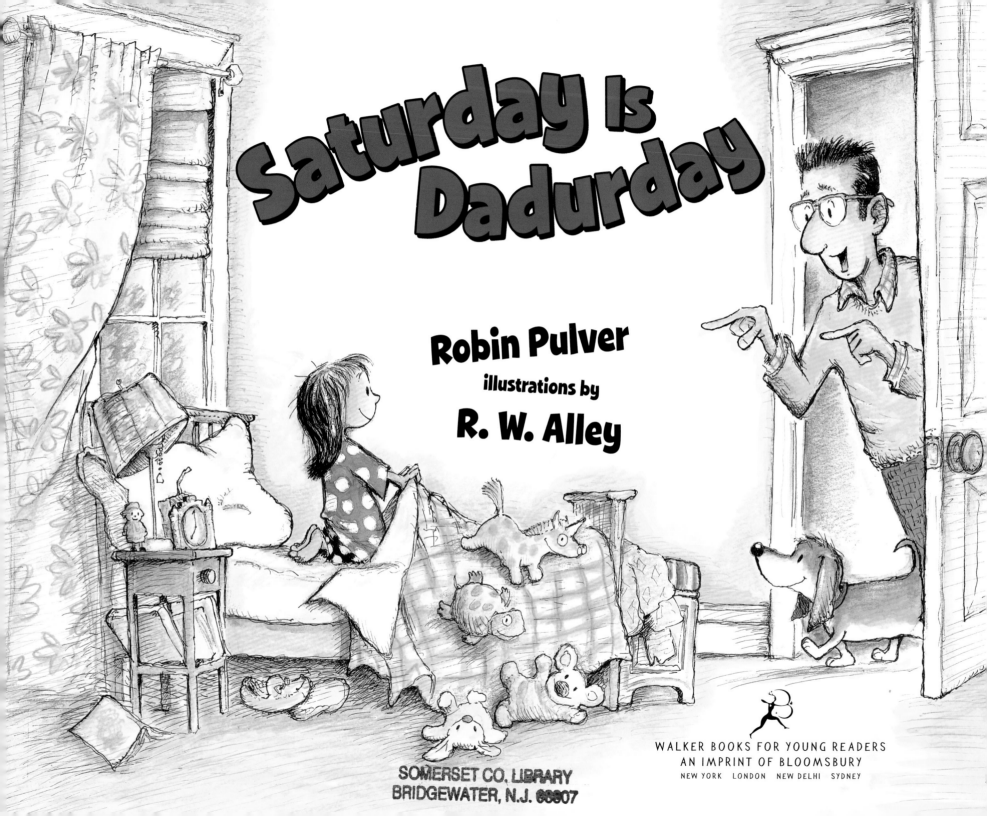

Saturday Is Dadurday

Robin Pulver

illustrations by

R. W. Alley

WALKER BOOKS FOR YOUNG READERS
AN IMPRINT OF BLOOMSBURY
NEW YORK   LONDON   NEW DELHI   SYDNEY

**For Grace Robin and
Charlotte Lucille . . . and their
Damaske dads! —R. P.**

Text copyright © 2013 by Robin Pulver
Illustrations copyright © 2013 by R. W. Alley

First published in the United States of America in May 2013
by Walker Books for Young Readers, an imprint of Bloomsbury Publishing, Inc.
www.bloomsbury.com

For information about permission to reproduce selections from this book, write to
Permissions, Walker BFYR, 175 Fifth Avenue, New York, New York 10010

Library of Congress Cataloging-in-Publication Data
Pulver, Robin.
Saturday is Dadurday / by Robin Pulver ; illustrated by R. W. Alley.
pages   cm
Summary: For Mimi, the best day of the week is always Saturday, the day she gets to spend with
just her dad. But when Dad's work takes him away from Mimi one Saturday, "Dadurday" is
ruined. Can Mimi find a way to save "Dadurday" and still make it special for her and her dad?
ISBN 978-0-8027-8691-3 (hardcover) • ISBN 978-0-8027-8609-8 (reinforced)
[1. Fathers—Fiction.] I. Alley, R. W., illustrator. II. Title.
PZ7.P97325Sat 2013   [E]—dc23   2012032293

Art created with watercolor, watercolor pencil, gouache, and pen and ink
Typeset in Centaur MT Std
Book design by Regina Roff

Printed in China by C&C Offset Printing Co., Ltd., Shenzhen, Guangdong
(hardcover) 10 9 8 7 6 5 4 3 2 1
(reinforced) 10 9 8 7 6 5 4 3 2 1

All papers used by Bloomsbury Publishing, Inc., are natural, recyclable products
made from wood grown in well-managed forests. The manufacturing processes
conform to the environmental regulations of the country of origin.

After the twins were born, Mimi and Dad had an idea for their same favorite day. It came after Friday, and Mimi and Dad called it **DADURDAY**.

Every Dadurday starts out the same way. Mimi and Dad make silly-shaped pancakes for breakfast.

They read the comic section of the newspaper.

Then they make lists of ideas for what to do on Dadurday.

On a sunny day, their lists might say:

"Uh-oh," says Dad. "No match!"

"I *meant* ride bikes to the library," Mimi explains. "That's a match!"

Go to the library

Play catch

Weed flower garden

Draw with chalk on the sidewalk

Play hide-and-seek

Ride bikes

On rainy days, their lists might say:

Play checkers
Repair bike
Splash in puddles

Splash in puddles
Play checkers
Have a party for stuffed animals

"It's a double match!" they say together.

Mimi always says, "Dadurday goes by too fast."

"Time flies when you're having fun," Dad agrees.

Then, one Friday evening, Dad says, "I'm so sorry to tell you this, Mimi, but I have to work on Saturdays from now on. I just found out today."

"What about Dadurday?" asks Mimi.

"It still will be Dadurday when I get home,"
says Dad. "We'll make the best of it."

"It won't be the same," moans Mimi.

Mimi was right.

In the morning there is no time for silly pancakes.

Mimi sulks. "This is **BADurday**!"

Reading the comics alone is no fun.

Mimi needs help with too many words.

"This is **MADurday**!" she grumbles.

Mimi makes a list of all she can think of:

Wait for Dad

Wait for Dad

Wait for Dad

"This is **SADurday**!" whines Mimi.

"Dad feels sad too," says Mom.

"Then he shouldn't go to work," Mimi complains.

"I'll play with you when the twins take their nap," says Mom.

Mimi wails, "Saturday can*not* be **MOMurday!**"

Mom sighs. "Well, it's not **MIMIday** either."

"Be like that," says Mimi. "And by the way, those twins don't even match."

Today *should* be **MIMIday**, thinks Mimi. Then Dad would *have* to stay home for me.

After lunch, Mimi waits for Dad. She
makes a list for when he comes home:

Piggyback ride
Play catch
Ride bikes

"Dad will be tired," Mom warns.
"I don't care," says Mimi.

Mimi watches the clock.
Time doesn't fly.

Time hardly moves at all.
It seems like time is taking a nap!
Mimi yawns.

She is tired of doing nothing.

She yawns again.

What if she and Dad are *both* too tired to do stuff when he gets home?

Mimi has to do something to make time fly.

She thinks and thinks.

Finally, Mimi has to admit, *Dadurday is* the best word for the day after Friday. Then Mimi has a good idea. Up and down the stairs she goes.

Down and up.

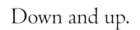

Outside and in.

Back and forth. Hurrying!

What if Dad comes home too soon?
Mimi forgets about being mad.
She forgets about being sad.

Dad calls to say he's on his way.
Now time is going too fast! Hurry!

Mom helps with silly-shaped pancakes.

Mimi makes party hats for the twins.

"I'm home!" says Dad.

"Surprise!" says Mimi.

"Wowee!" says Dad. "All this for me?"

"Who else?" asks Mimi. "It's **DADurday**!"

"I love you, Mimi!" says Dad.
"I love you too, Dad," says Mimi.
And that is the best match of all.